Third Instar

David Gullen

Third Instar
by David Gullen
ISBN: 978-1-908125-69-9

Cover Art by David Rix

Publication Date: March 2019

EibonVale
Press

1

Mazehew left the high-ceilinged rail terminus when he saw the gendarme's red bonnet. He sat on the kerb near the taxi rank, smoked a cigarette from his tin and watched the station clock.

His clothes were old but cared for: a battered traveller's hat and maroon waistcoat, baggy sand-stained trousers, decent boots. A plain gold ring hung from his ear, three days' stubble on his jaw. A patched and faded elan clung to him as false as his accent.

The city had a coastal feel, the reach of the sky deeper in one direction than the other. From the railway terminus to the great square called Kala Agr, all along the tree-lined Avenue of Princes with its petrified gods, down through the dusty souks and narrow lanes, the entire city faced the boundless skies beyond the Grand Parade. The place the whole world called the Edge.

An inbound train arrived, a surge of tourists spilled down the terminus steps. Acrid blue smoke plumed from the two-stroke taxis. Male and female hawkers worked the crowd. They sold nuts and juice, kite rides, sweetmeats, pterodactyl finger bones, black lotus, themselves.

Mazehew spotted a tired couple with two young children. He roused himself and went to work.

That evening he connected with a lone traveller, a waif-girl from the cities of the central plains. He'd had an unsuccessful day – nobody had needed escorting to their hotel or wanted a guided tour of the town or a trip to the iron cauldron.

She was dark and slender with a hint of a frown across her brow. The hem of her long skirts swept the dusty ground, the sleeves of her purple top hung below her fingers.

She stood in front of a waffle stand with a coin in her upraised hand. Other people came and went, she stood like a statue in the shifting crowd. Mazehew had seldom seen anyone so unnoticed. It was almost as if the world had forgotten she was there – almost. A young man with bad skin and a wisp of beard stared fixedly at the open bag on her shoulder. Mazehew observed with interest.

The young man sidled forwards, his attention falsely and obviously directed elsewhere. Close behind the woman he looked guiltily around.

Mazehew's mouth twisted with contempt – an amateur. He closed the gap in the three long strides, seized the man's wrist and yanked his arm into the air. "I don't think so!"

"Let me go! What are you doing?" The man twisted in his grip, all injured indignity. Mazehew smoothly palmed the purse in the woman's bag with his other hand.

"I saw him," the waffle-seller shouted at Mazehew. "Pickpocket."

The city lived on tourism. Stall-holders and passers-by surrounded the thief in a bad-tempered crowd.

Mazehew put his hand under the woman's elbow, touching but not holding. "Madam, come with me please. Quickly."

She blinked, startled, and lowered her arm. "What's the matter? Am I in trouble?"

"Not at all. Please – this way."

He deftly steered her into the nearby souk, released her and stood back. Most of the evening crowd surrounded the pick-pocket but Mazehew knew the rest watched him.

She studied him warily. "What do you want?"

"There was a thief." He gestured at her shoulder. "Your bag –"

She stared wide-eyed then dug frantically through her bag. "No, no. Not again –"

Mazehew proffered the red purse. "Is this yours?"

"Yes!" She checked the contents and looked up in happy disbelief. "It's all here. Oh, thank you!"

Mazehew smiled. He held out his hand. "I'm Mazehew."

She briefly held his fingers. "Frayel. I – thank you so much." She looked past him to the food stalls. "I just wanted –"

"There are better places to eat."

Emotions burned in Frayel's eyes: betrayal, disappointment, relief. "I need a drink. Let me buy you one." She had a lopsided smile. "People say you shouldn't drink alone."

Mazehew pulled off his battered had and ran his hand through thinning hair. "I could use one, I don't confront thieves every day."

He made her smile, she made him laugh. She bought him a drink, then another. Frayel was easy company. On impulse, Mazehew took her to his favourite cafeteria deep in the old town – half a dozen square tables with plain white tablecloths, each with a jam jar holding a single marigold. They ate braised lamb cooked with spices from the bazaar and vegetables from the old market. Mazehew relaxed in the lamp-lit atmosphere rich with warmth from the kitchen and tinged with tobacco smoke. This was a place he kept for himself, for pleasure. He never played his plays or talked the talk here. The owners enjoyed his custom, the regulars his dubious company.

Frayel was lonely in the ways that someone who has travelled long and far can be. Mazehew worked his ordinary charms and let the magic of the city and the café's food and wine weave their spells.

After they had eaten she grew introspective. Her soft voice became strong. "Were you looking for me?"

"How could I be?" Mazehew leaned back in his chair and sipped his wine. Sweet and soft, it was the best in the café and surprisingly good. Wine Frayel had insisted on buying.

She touched his hand, understanding, accepting. "I mean someone like me."

"I wasn't –" Mazehew halted mid-protest, confused by his own motivations. "No," he said firmly. "Call it fate, kismet, what you will, our paths simply crossed."

She bit her lip and smiled, turned the stem of her wine glass between her fingers. Self-consciousness returned; she looked away. "We all dree our own weird."

"What is that?" Mazehew said with a puzzled laugh.

She lifted his fingertips to her lips. "To follow your fate and do what must be done."

"Were you born here?" Frayel lay nude on her bed, one leg over the side, her hair over one shoulder, unselfconscious in the afterglow. Mazehew's one real talent was bringing physical pleasure.

"I was travelling like you. Somehow I just stayed."

"Why?"

If he had known the answer she wanted, he would have told her. He pulled aside the curtain and looked down into the narrow lane. He considered lying. Truth was seldom easy. "I ran out of reasons to leave."

Which was not the half of it. Not the happy childhood or the bright self-centred student. Neither his dissatisfaction with convention nor its rejection. Certainly not the slow slide from seeker to drifter to – whatever he had become.

Her faint frown had returned. She traced a vein along the inside of her forearm "There are always reasons to leave."

Frayel was beautiful. Mazehew did not understand.

The next day they went to the bazaar. Mazehew gently steered Frayel to the stalls where he had an arrangement with the owner. The goods were from the same workshops, what difference did it make?

All through the various quarters, Frayel felt the drape of the silks and cottons, tried to open the magic boxes, and peered into bins of snails and baby tortoises. She admired the gold and silverwork, the lamp-smiths, the spices heaped like coloured volcanoes. At each stall she smiled and moved on. Behind her, Mazehew and the stall holders exchanged looks of quiet exasperation.

It was only at the kite-makers that she showed real interest, fascinated by the animal, bird, and flower-designs of the big kites hanging from the rafters by their guy lines.

Mazehew had no relationship with any of the kite-makers. He leaned against the jamb of the entrance and rolled a cigarette.

Frayel looked up at a huge kite in the shape of a midnight-blue swift with wing-tips and tail trimmed in white.

"The night-swift is a man-kite." The shop assistant was dressed in a kite-flyer's close-fitting black tights and vest. He tried to turn Frayel towards the smaller kites. His hip brushed against hers. "Mayfly and marigold kites, very pretty designs."

Frayel returned to the night swift. "I like this one."

"It is for a man, someone of heavier build." A waft of tobacco smoke drew his attention to Mazehew silhouetted in the entrance. "Perhaps your –?"

"My friend." Frayel smiled at Mazehew. "My good friend."

Mazehew pinched out his cigarette and strolled inside. His arm slipped around Frayel's waist, he kissed her cheek. "Are you going to buy one?"

"Perhaps." Her eyes lost focus, her voice dreamy. "Would you watch me fly? Come out there with me –?"

Mazehew didn't like the Grand Parade where the kite-men flew beyond the Edge. He didn't like the sky beyond the railings, a sky that reached up and out and also down. He didn't like the utter absence of ground inches from his feet, the way the blue air faded to stars in the evening, up and out and also down. Most of all he didn't like how the Edge made him feel – small, like nothing. Insignificant.

"Yes," Mazehew said. "Of course I will."

The kite seller hung a harness over Frayel's chest. He tightened the straps around her thighs, he explaining how the D-rings at shoulder, waist and leg secured her to the kite and left her arms free to control the winch.

Frayel spoke in an awed whisper. "Just imagine … Floating on air, suspended over –"

The kite seller's eyes gleamed. "Infinity."

"What if the rope breaks?"

"Our ropes are very strong."

Frayel looked into some inner space. "I don't want this, it's …" She opened the buckles, stepped out of the harness and hung it over the counter.

Out on the street Mazehew suggested she ride in a tethered balloon. "They are very safe, I know one of the operators."

"Take me back into town. I want to the see the smoke-dancers and the stone gods."

"They're not made of stone." Mazehew said sharply then immediately regretted his tone. "Everyone thinks that at first."

Frayel bought roast nuts and cinnamon *lokma* from street vendors. They ate them as they walked, licking the honey from their fingers. At the Avenue of Princes, they wandered between the petrified gods under the high canopies of ancient chestnut and blue beech. Part animal, part human, the gods were big as houses. Some crouched, others reared with their arms and other limbs upraised.

"They look scared," Frayel said. "What could scare them?"

"Some say it is adoration."

One massive form was sleekly graceful, with a fan of dorsal flukes. Frayel laid her palm against the hexagonal plates along the flank. Her eyes widened, the armoured surface looked like grey-blue stone but had the texture of leather. "It's warm. She's warm."

"They are not stone," Mazehew said gently. He laid his head against the goddess. "Listen."

Frayel put her ear to the goddess's side and heard the same sounds Mazehew first heard many years ago: a soft rushing like wind in trees, a ponderous kettle-drum beat.

Frayel looked up in awe. "They are not dead."

"If they ever truly lived." Mazehew pointed down the avenue to where one of the Gods was framed in scaffolding. "A hereditary guild cares for them."

The Gods grew stranger closer to the Edge with baroque horns and fins, asymmetric hybrids of human, animal, and *other*. Here the avenue widened as both buildings and trees drew away from the extravagant, disturbing forms. Frayel looked up at a rearing elephantine thing with a tentacle face, jointed arms and five unequal legs. She shivered under the late afternoon sun. "I'm glad we came here in daylight. At night –?" She hugged herself and shivered again.

As dusk drew down, they ate at Zapotek's, the roof café overlooking Kala Agr square. Once again Frayel insisted on paying. Mazehew picked at the chipped edge of their table with his thumbnail. "Let me buy the wine. The most expensive isn't always the best."

"Thank you."

Mazehew's heart lifted. "You're welcome."

As they ate, darkness fell and stars spread across the sky from the endless night far beyond the Edge. All across the ancient square, storytellers lit their yellow torches. A circle of listeners gathered round each one, dark rings around pools of light.

"Do you want to go down?" Mazehew said.

"How long have the story-tellers been here?"

"A thousand years."

"Then they will be here tomorrow." Frayel leaned back into her chair. "The petrified Gods were eerie things. When I shut my eyes I can still see them. Until the dancers come, I just want to look at the stars, smell the spices in the air and drink wine with you."

An hour passed. The voices of the storytellers and their drums and gongs came up faint from the square. Mazehew and Frayel shared tales of life and past loves.

When the dongle and rattle of tin cups and chains said that the wine sellers had arrived, Mazehew led Frayel down the stairs then through an open crowd across Kala Agr.

The storytellers had gone; everyone was buying hot spiced wine. The nearest wine-seller was a cheerful and almost toothless young man. Dented tin cups hung from chains attached to the urn on his back. He filled two and Mazehew paid him.

"The spices are part of the dance. They help you see into the smoke and feel the dance with your body."

Most people asked if it was addictive. Frayel simply pulled down her cuff and took the hot cup.

The wine was pungent and syrup-sweet. Under the cinnamon, molasses, cloves and nutmeg was an aftertaste – something bitter, an earthy taint. She sipped again and whispered, "What happened to the wine seller's teeth?"

"At the end of the night, they drink what they don't sell. The sugar rots their teeth."

"Why don't they make less wine?"

Something softly broke inside Mazehew. He wanted to hug her. "I don't think that's the point."

"Oh." Frayel said, then laughed. "Oh!"

Only the locals and people like Mazehew noticed the smoke dancers arrive – a nondescript group of stocky men and women wearing dark trousers and plain smocks.

Mazehew finished his wine, let go of the cup and watched it swing back on its chain with fascinating slowness. The cup hit the others hanging there and a moment later he heard the sound. The whole world moved at three-quarter speed.

Silver grey smoke rose in a wall across one side of the square. Fans of shadow and light swung through the smoke as it rose higher and higher. The smoke-dancers danced, simple silhouettes of ordinary men and women. The shadows-shapes grew and grew. One by one they disrobed and danced as beautiful naked giants. Shadow feet left the ground, the dancers floated into the sky. Silver smoke arched over Kala Agr like a curved shell.

Frayel clutched Mazehew's hand. "This is wonderful. How do they do it?"

Mazehew had seen it all before, many times. "Which?"

"Any of it. All."

He whispered like an enchanted child. "I don't know."

The smoke drew back into an extra dimension, no longer a wall but a place. In the far distance, enormous shapes swam closer. A pulse of awe moved through the gathered crowd. Mazehew and Frayel saw the shapes for what they were – the Gods from the Avenue of Princes. Among them flew the finned half-human goddess Frayel had touched.

The shadow-dancers rose higher and embraced the gods, coupled with them.

Frayel's feet left the ground. She hung on to Mazehew. "I can fly," she exulted. "We can join them. Come with me."

Mazehew wanted nothing more. His blood sang, his body was left behind. Together they rose into the air.

Afterwards there was nothing but a crowd of people under a midnight sky. The dancers, the smoke, and the Gods were gone. Strangers looked at each other and smiled.

Frayel danced in the sparse torchlight, her eyes shone. "One great leap –" She flung her hand up to the sky "– and I could be there."

Mazehew felt the same breathless ache. "Would you?"

"Yes." She looked at him steadily. "Would you?"

He was filled with a rare peace. "Yes."

Frayel kissed him passionately, she pressed her body against his. "Give me a night like last night. Make this a perfect day."

Later, in their room:

"Did you hear the singing? Like birds and angels."

"Yes," Mazehew said. There had been no music, yet he had its memory.

In the morning Mazehew woke before Frayel. He drew the curtains and looked out the window at an overcast sky. A steady wind blew towards the Edge – kite weather.

Halfway through making tea, Mazehew looked at Frayel asleep in the bed and wondered what he was doing. His hat was on the chair, his coat hung on the door, Frayel's purse lay on the dresser. A remnant of last night's peace remained. He pushed the thoughts aside, knelt beside the bed and stroked her hair. Frayel stretched sleepily.

Mazehew kissed her brow. "Time to wake up. The kite wind is blowing."

Immediately Frayel was wide awake. Her eyes fixed on his. "I have to be there."

Mazehew fetched her tea then pushed up the window. As usual it stuck halfway. He thumped it on the right side and it slid open. Down in the lane, all the movement was in one direction. Tourists, buskers, hawkers and pedlars, businessmen and women, all made their way towards the Grand Parade. Kite weather – even Mazehew felt a reluctant buzz. Pairs of figures dressed in white mingled with the crowd, the volunteer guardians who patrolled Grand Parade.

He sipped his tea and brooded, deeply equivocal about visiting the Edge. Why had he mentioned the wind? He put down his cup. This was for Frayel. This was something he could do for her.

By the time they arrived, kites hung on their frames all along the parade. Each one was different: a bird or fish, snakes, flowers, one was like an open book. Kite riders pretended to ignore the growing crowd as they buckled themselves to their kites. One by one they faced the offland wind, slipped their tethers and lofted into the air under snapping fluttering fabric and creaking struts.

"There's the night swift," Frayel said.

It was the young kite-man from the shop. The black-winged kite rose out over the Edge and hung in the air on a short line. He released the brake on his chest-winch, line spooled out and the black swift lofted him up and away into the empty blue beyond the Edge. It was all Mazehew could do to watch.

Frayel griped the top bar of the railings. Kite lines thrummed as taut as steel cables, dwindling to cobweb threads. "Imagine hanging there and never dropping. In front of you – the entire world."

Beside her, Mazehew imagined that vast space very well. He knees shook. At night you could look down on constellations.

"Imagine if you had a rope long enough to see the world's corners."

"Go too far out and the wind fails," Mazehew said.

"What if it blew forever?"

"The rope would break under its own weight."

"You've seen this?"

Mazehew wanted to say, *Yes, I was there when it happened, I saw the line part, so distant it seemed inconsequential. I saw how it hung in curves like a serpent then flick back faster and faster. I heard the whip-crack as the line lashed across the Grand Parade. I saw it score stone and cut metal, saw it decapitate Arnolds the waiter.*

On that day, the shriek of the winches as the kites came in sounded like screams all along the Grand Parade. Behind them one kite floated further and further away, a scrap of fabric and struts and one lone lost figure. It passed beyond the wind's reach, dipped once, twice, and was gone.

Mazehew shook his head. "I didn't see it. I only heard."

Some said the line had been cut.

Further down the parade, a lively group of young men leaned over the rail and flipped pennies into the air. Across the way men and women in business suits sat in the street cafés, ordered croissants and coffee and never looked at the distant kites.

A tall and raw-boned woman and a thick-set man walked over to the group. Both wore white trousers and shirts and carried canvas satchels over their shoulders. The woman handed them a pamphlet and spoke briefly. The men listened, grew sober, and stepped down from the rail.

"Who are they?" Frayel said.

"Guardians. Volunteers, watching out for –" Mazehew didn't want to say, "– certain people."

On an impulse Mazehew bought Frayel a pendant of a night swift from one of the street hawkers. The outspread silver-wire wings and tail feathers were inlaid with black enamel, the bird's head turned to one side showed one elegant white eye. It was a lovely thing and more expensive than he expected.

Frayel was delighted. She fastened the chain around her neck, the swift hung inside her blouse. She unfastened a button, then another, exposing the bird and the tops of her breasts. "There, now everyone can see."

"They can indeed," Mazehew smiled.

She stroked the swift with her finger tip. "Let them. It is beautiful, I will never take it off."

"You are beautiful too, Frayel," Mazehew blurted out. Inner agony consumed him. Too much too soon? What a fool. He meant it.

Frayel's eyes were on the distant kites, her palm over the pendant. "If I could fly …"

She hadn't heard him. Mazehew felt relief and disappointment in equal amounts.

"Where now?" Frayel said.

There was only one thing left to see, a mile down the parade along the Edge. This he could do for her.

"The cauldron." He held out his hand, she took it. They ducked under the kite lines and walked away from the town to the rickety stalls of the old market. The level paving turned to old cobbles and older brick, the iron railing along the Edge ended, a waist-high wall of weathered white granite began.

The market thronged with local folk buying and selling produce. Out beyond the stalls a black iron cauldron twenty feet across half-blocked the old parade. The cauldron rested on a central boss, tilted towards and over the Edge through a gap in the wall. Three huge chains with links as thick through as Mazehew's wrist ran loosely from iron hoops set around the cauldron's rim across the ground and down into a cleft in the solid rock. It was an old thing, older than city.

Frayel was fascinated. Her hand drifted over the age-pitted metal. "This is so strange. In my mind there is an echo, a memory of a journey …"

Mazehew skirted the cauldron uneasily. It was a weirdling thing, less a container than a way to display whatever it once held to the sky. He stubbed his toe on one of the chains and stumbled. "Seen enough?"

"Almost."

A sparrow-boned old man came from the market with a wicker basket. He was barefoot, with cataracts filming his eyes and skin wrinkled like leather. The basket shook as he held it out to show the oranges and apples inside. It was good fruit.

"I'm sorry, I've spent all my money," Frayel told the fruit seller.

Mazehew pulled his pockets inside out. "Me too."

The old man picked an orange from his basket. "Take this, a gift for love. I'm not so blind I can't see."

They were being watched from the market. Mazehew knew the spiel. "I really do have no money."

The old man smiled. Despite his age, his teeth were good. He still held out the orange. "I know."

Not wanting to upset him, Mazehew took the fruit and bowed. "My thanks. Long life, happiness."

Frayel went to where the rim overhung the Edge through the gap in the wall. Wind whistled through the gap sucking fragments of grit into the sky. Mazehew hung back.

"Out there – is that a pterodactyl colony?"

Half-way into blue distance, the land rose into peaks and crags, the outer edge fell sheer beyond sight. Above the cliff, a cluster of dark specks gyred, dipped, and swung over airy nothing.

"Glide-wing riders from the out-of-town resorts."

"I'd liked to have seen a pterodactyl."

"The wind is wrong for them here."

They watched the riders in silence.

"They look so free."

Just the thought of what those men and women were doing made Mazehew's skin crawl. "They are that," he conceded.

Frayel stood close against him, her chin on his chest. She looked so solemn he kissed her brow.

"Mazehew. When I go, will you come with me?"

This was strange. In the past Mazehew simply took what he could get and moved on leaving lies and broken promises. This time he … He and Frayel … This was strange. He had never lied to her.

"When are you going?"

She breathed deep. "Now?"

It occurred to Mazehew there was nothing for him here. A rented room, his old clothes, a few associates and no true friends. With Frayel, a fresh start together. A chance to be a different man, a better man. He wanted it.

"All right." As he spoke an enormous weight lifted. "Yes."

She lifted her pendant so the swallow swung on its chain. "I'm ready. When you gave me this, I knew."

Mazehew realised she was right. "So did I."

Frayel swung up onto the balustrade in a single fluid motion.

Mazehew stared at her, his heart in his mouth. "Be careful."

Frayel kicked off her shoes. They tumbled over the Edge and were gone. She spread her arms like a bird, a swallow. Her toes gripped the outer edge of the stonework. She called to Mazehew. "Come, my darling. Together we'll be free and fly!"

In one ice-cold moment Mazehew understood how he had been wrong. His brain ground to a halt, he could not move. Across the way the chatter in the market died. Far down the promenade two figures in white hurried towards them.

Mazehew's mind lurched back into action. "Frayel, stop, wait."

She held out her hand behind her. "Now is the time. Come with me, soar like the swifts."

Mazehew tried to speak, to swallow. His tongue stuck in his mouth, he coughed a panicked breath. "Wait, I'm coming."

Half petrified he clambered onto the wall. The old granite felt slick under his clammy hands. He swayed into a half-crouch, took one wavering step and tilted out over giddy nothing. *Gods and dancers – Save me.*

His arms spread wide Mazehew shuffled towards Frayel. The wind pushed, the void pulled. He moaned in distress. "Wait, Frayel."

Frayel threw back her head and spread her arms like wings.

The two figures in white raced towards them, satchels flying.

Mazehew clutched Frayel around the waist. "Frayel, listen. This isn't what I want. I want you, I want life."

Frayel twisted round and tried to embrace him. Her eyes burned with golden light. "This is life. This is the ultimate. We'll fall and fly. We'll couple like the Gods. You shall ride me and I, you –"

"No, Frayel," Mazehew pleaded. "Not like this. Come down."

The glow went from Frayel's eyes, a red light burned. "You promised. You lied."

"No." The accusation stung, his grip loosened. She pushed out, he leaned back. They teetered over the edge.

"Everybody lies!"

She fought to be free with reckless strength. He tried to hold her. The moment came when he had to let go or follow her down.

Frayel hung off-balance. She whirled her arms. "Mazehew!"

He clutched at her shirt. Cloth tore, his finger snagged the swallow pendant, the light chain went taut. Frayel hung in the air, reaching. The chain parted and she was gone.

Off-balance, Mazehew howled. Not this, not now. In madness he wanted to follow. His legs pushed back, his arms flailed, his body wanted to live.

Hands yanked him backwards. He fell hard, smashed his check on stone and collapsed half-stunned against the wall. An agitated crowd gathered. One of the Guardians gathered him up, the raw-boned woman. Her voice was strong but gentle, "This is no answer, there is always a better choice."

Overwhelmed and half-stunned Mazehew looked into the Guardian's dark eyes. Words welled inside but his tongue would not move. Gingerly he touched his broken cheek and saw red blood on his fingers.

"It's all right. Take your time." The Guardian spoke up. "Does anyone know this man?"

A voice came out of the crowd, hard and unsympathetic. "He's a street-sharp, a false guide."

The male Guardian helped him stand. Dazed and sick Mazehew slowly straightened, his cheek cupped in his palm. Blood dripped through his fingers and tap-tapped onto his boots.

Another voice came: "He pushed her."

The Guardian's grip on Mazehew tightened. "Say this is not true."

"No." Shock, pain, loss, it was hard to think. "I tried … I didn't …"

"He stole her brooch," someone shouted.

"In his hand."

"Thief."

"Murderer."

The crowd pushed forwards. "Give him to us."

"I bought it for her," Mazehew protested. Even to himself it sounded false.

"A con-man like you?"

"He pushed her."

"I saw him."

"And I."

An apple flew through the air and hit Mazehew's brow. The shock was worse than the pain. A flurry of missiles flew through the air, potatoes, apples, turnips. Hard things. Mazehew didn't understand.

The Guardians pushed in front of him. The man held up his arms. "Listen to me. Even if what you say is true, this is not the way."

The crowd morphed into a mob, a beast with a dozen mouths. "He'll lie." "We saw." "They'll just fine him." "We saw what happened." "Give Him To Us."

Belatedly Mazehew realised how much trouble he was in. They wanted his blood, he had seen what mobs could do.

Clawing hands reached for the Guardians. Angry, they slapped them away. More hands grabbed, fingers hooked, fists raised. The woman broke free. *Go, go!* she mouthed at Mazehew, white with fear and twice as determined. She faced the mob. "Leave us be. We are Guardians."

Mazehew backed away, Frayel's pendant forgotten in his fist.

"They're helping him escape!"

The mob flowed over the struggling Guardians. Mazehew broke into a shambling run. Behind him came a high shriek, an awful wet tearing sound. Terror gripped his legs.

Missiles slammed into Mazehew's back. The great cauldron blocked his path. He tried to cut inland and four young men headed him off, cold-eyed and feral. Wildly, Mazehew wondered where such hate came from.

He backed away, tripped and fetched up against the gap in the wall. Wind whistled through his clothes. The crowd bayed like a hunting pack, a flurry of missiles battered him. He slid under the cauldron, his legs hung over empty space with the wind pushing, pushing.

Something dizzyingly struck his head. He slid further back. A few more inches and he'd be gone, down and down after Frayel.

Franticly Mazehew writhed and kicked. The pendant slipped from his grip. He snatched one end of the broken chain and watched helplessly as it slid off the other end and dropped into the void. Moaning with fear, he writhed and kicked. He braced one foot against the wall, hauled himself up and tumbled head-first inside the cauldron. He scrabbled up into the lee of the upper rim. A futile few seconds respite before they hauled him out.

Under his weight the cauldron ponderously crumped down onto stone. The mob yelled with one great fearful voice as the cauldron slid towards the edge dragging the three chains behind it. Far underground, a slow clank-clink-clank of ratchets began as more links emerged from the cleft.

The cauldron tilted over the edge. Mazehew tumbled across the floor and slammed bruisingly into the lower rim. All he could see was sky – up forever, out forever, down forever. Overhead the crowd screamed like a beast denied its prey.

Rock crumbled and the cauldron dropped ten feet out from under him. In a moment of unnatural clarity, just as he felt his innards rise, he thought: *This cannot be happening to me. This is not real. How did my life come to this?* And he also knew his mind was too calm for such a dreadful moment, calm in a way that teetered on its own wild edge. Another great shout came from the crowd and he was astonished to find he could hear every separate voice.

The chains snapped tight and he thumped down onto the iron floor. Smashed, stunned, overwhelmed, Mazehew lay on his back and stared glassily up. A row of faces peered over the parapet. Every one of them was pleased to see him gone and glad they were here to see it.

The cauldron sank steadily down. The clank-clink-clank of the underground ratchets faded, a wall of weathered rock slid past. It seemed to Mazehew that he stayed still while the world rose up and away.

The ancient fruit-seller appeared at the parapet. He upended his basket and oranges tumbled into the cauldron.

The faces in the crowd blurred into one. Slow and unstoppable the cauldron continued to descend. An appalling terror welled up inside Mazehew. More than anything he wanted to be home, be a child again, to be forgiven and held in his mother's arms. He curled up on his side and shrieked.

Time passed, or he passed by time. It became that he did not know. No longer knew. Had never known. The wall slid upwards in twisted bands of white, grey, ochre, green and black stone, some narrow, some wide as days. Once in a while the rock face ran wet. Flat ribbons of green scale clung there, branching and dividing.

He stared blankly at the cliff wall hour after hour. Sometimes it receded a few feet, sometimes the cauldron bumped and scraped against it. When the rock was close enough to touch, he let it drag past his fingers until their tips were rubbed raw. He followed the parallel bloody streaks up the rock with eyes that understood damage but not pain.

It was easier to think of the rock rising than him descending, easier to watch the rock rise than look in any other direction and see nothing but empty air, oceans of cloud. At night, the stars.

The cauldron descended in a series of smooth bumps, one for every link of chain, a rhythm like a heartbeat. The ratchet clink was long gone. When he put his ear against one of the chains he heard the groan and creak of metal torsion.

He dreamed he tried to climb the chain, climbed forever as it lowered him at the exact rate he could climb. Exhausted, he fell – and woke gasping in the cauldron. His fingertips were scabbed with black blood and burned like fire, his tongue clung to the roof of his mouth.

Vegetable missiles littered the cauldron, among them seven good oranges. He peeled one, the citrus stung his fingertips. He squeezed juice into his mouth until his tongue unstuck, the juice sharp on his cracked lips, tasteless in his mouth. One at a time he licked his fingers clean. Flavour came then, sweetly intense, blissfully sad. He broke the orange into segments and ate them slowly and cried without tears.

Some part of him said this was self-pity. He spat the seeds into his hand. His fingers hurt. His remembered his name. He blinked and looked around. Here he was.

Mazehew tipped the orange pips into his pocket and took an inventory:

Water – None

Apples – Three. All bruised

Sweet potatoes – Also three. Two large, one small.

Cabbage – One. Old and half rotten

Oranges – Seven. Six uneaten.

He tore away the dead parts from the cabbage and dropped them over the side. Everything else he put in a neat row along one side of the cauldron. About to throw the orange peel away he hesitated. If it came to that, he could eat it.

His mouth twisted, who was he fooling with "If"? He thought about Frayel then, of what she had done and why, and where she was now. He wondered who she had really been and what had made her that way and concluded he knew little and understood less. An emotional pivot swung inside him. He leaned on the cauldron wall looked down and down and thought about joining her. Too soon. He laughed, a raw cracked sound, the first he had made since going over the edge. There was plenty of time, his options were open.

Now he accepted what was happening, it was he who descended and the cliff that stayed still. Rock spread up, down, left and right, a vertical infinity in two dimensions. High overhead the three chains dwindled and vanished. Mazehew knew leagues-long chains should break under their own weight. Perhaps he was dead and this was – what? Even if that was true, it meant nothing, it changed nothing.

He ate only when he could no longer not eat, and voided his waste over the edge. He ate the bruised apples first, flesh, core and seeds. Always the wall of rock slid by.

Water was his great problem. He sucked at damp seeps when the wall was close. When there was a running flow he used cabbage leaves for cups.

One time, the wall drew away and a cataract poured from a horizontal slash in the rock. A broad ribbon of glassy water fell soundlessly then broke into curtains of spray. Mazehew stared in disbelief. So much water, so close yet out of reach. He tried to swing the cauldron, running from one side to the other on legs that creaked and ached with disuse. He found the rhythm and by fractions and inches the cauldron began to move. Oranges and sweet potato rolled across the floor. Mazehew heaved and lunged but no matter how hard he tried the cauldron would only swing so far and no more. Water fell a yard beyond his reach. Sobbing and swearing Mazehew hung off the chains at the peak of each swing then dashed back to the other side. At full pelt his turned his foot on a sweet potato and was half over the side before he knew it. He hung from his elbow crooked round a chain, looked down at his legs dangling over infinity and yelled in cold terror. Shaking with fright, he hauled himself back into the cauldron.

The falling water spread into mist and rain. For an hour, he descended through a clinging drizzle that saturated his hair and clothes. Marvelling at his own stupidity he stripped, wrung grey water out of his clothes and let them soak again. He sucked water from the sopping cloth until he felt bloated. He squeezed water out of his hair, rubbed his face and body and felt clean again. Sated, he sat in the dripping mist with his eyes closed. He stretched, laughed and shook his head. What a fool; he had nearly killed himself with a potato.

The cauldron continued its descent and the mist dissipated. Five good oranges and one sweet potato bobbed in three inches of scummy water. Mazehew tore a sleeve from his shirt and tied off one end. He dropped the oranges and potato inside and knotted the sleeve to one of the chains. When the rest of his clothes had dried, he dressed and tied his shoes to another of the chains by their laces.

The water sloshing in the cauldron was undrinkable, sleep would be unpleasant. Mazehew looked down at his body. Always thin, now he was gaunt. *Not too long now*, he thought. *Not long at all.*

In a moment of inspiration, he groped underwater for the central floor boss, gripped it with both hands and twisted. It moved through a quarter-turn and came free. Gurgling and sucking, the filthy water drained away. Mazehew smiled to himself and replaced the boss. The floor was clean, his shoes were drying on their string, food hung in his makeshift larder; the cauldron felt almost homely. The thought filled him with a satisfaction so deep he knew it was unreasonable. So be it. Happiness lived where you found it. He took the last sweet potato from his sleeve bag, sat against the cauldron wall and contentedly gnawed it.

Time passed. The smallest effort exhausted him. He slept five more times. Each time he woke, he ate one of the remaining oranges, stripped the pithy fibre from the inside of the peel and put the seeds in his pocket.

Sleep and wakefulness blurred. Mazehew lay in the cauldron day after day. He remembered his childhood and his student days, the years of dissatisfaction and wandering, his time as a petty predator in the city by the Edge. Insight came – all the causes of his discontent came from within.

A change in the ambient sound tugged at him. At first a hollow echo accompanied the bump and scrape of the cauldron down the endless cliff, then – silence. Mazehew opened his eyes expecting to see the rock face had moved a few feet back. Instead he looked into the roof of a great cave.

His heart lurched in his mouth and he cried out, a feeble croak. He crawled across the cauldron on aching joints and leaned on the side. The cave was wide and high, a dim cathedral of grey shadow that ran deep into the world, its furthest reaches vanished into murk.

Through all the days and miles of his descent, this was the first cave he had seen. He was near the end of his strength, this was his last, his only chance to escape. The cauldron sank slowly down; the cave floor was still several minutes descent away. He gauged the distance from the cauldron to the cave mouth as a dozen feet. A risky jump at the best of times and far beyond him now.

There was time, he could leave. His shoes still hung on the chain, cracked and dry. He pulled them free, whirled them over his head and hurled them at the cave. His aim as true, they lay there in the grey dust, waiting.

He set the cauldron swinging, found the rhythm and set the pace. He was lighter and weaker than before and the cauldron responded slowly. Back and forth, back and forth, he broke the cauldron's inertia by inches and degrees. Yet each time he looked into cavern he felt the depth of the silence that emanated there, a silence that reached out and seeped into his bones. His enthusiasm faltered and died. The cauldron creaked and swayed and sank down. Ten feet above the floor Mazehew looked deep into the cavern. Light only penetrated so far but he saw vastly further into a region of colourless light, a silent motionless infinity that ran on and branched and spread forever.

He no longer wanted to look but found he could not turn away. And although he did not want to, he started to rock the cauldron again, tottering back and forth to bring the cave mouth closer. All the while he stared fixedly into the grey lamps of the cave-light and felt the silence of ash and dust creep further inside him. His breath rasped, his heartbeat faltered, his eyesight dimmed. He howled at his legs to stop but they would not stop. The cave light compelled them.

When he fell, his body felt boneless, the floor of the iron cauldron soft. Grateful his rebellious body had finally failed, he looked up at the cave while his legs twitched and spasmed. The cauldron sank further down and he could no longer see into the cave. Free of its gaze, his will returned. His mouth twisted into a rictus of relief before his calves cramped into agonies. Hissing in pain, he forced his legs straight, lay gasping, then closed his eyes and slept.

When he woke the cauldron had descended into a region of milky cloud. There was no sky, no dwindling chain, just the cauldron and the cliff and the occasional hollow bang as they came together.

He lay with his feet towards the rock face and watched it slide past. The dimensions rotated so he felt that he stood and the cauldron floor was a wall against his back, the cliff the ground sliding by under his feet. He could walk out of here, walk home. All it would take was one step…

Mazehew closed his eyes. His body had betrayed him at the cave, now it was his mind. All would end here, in the cauldron and not the cave. With that he was content.

2

He woke with rain pattering on his face and lay still, feeling each soft impact on his skin and dimpling his ragged clothes. The familiar motion of the cauldron had ceased. He heard bird song and opened his eyes.

Swifts wheeled and cried overhead. A wet wind blew and with it came a distant chatter of normal conversation, the rustling swell of trees. Confused and unsteady, Mazehew peered over the cauldron's edge. His mind swam; he was back on the flagstones of the Grand Parade. Half a mile to the left, the city rose; in the other direction, crags piled in the far distance. Across the way were the awnings and hand-written signs of the vegetable market.

Mazehew crawled over the rim and tumbled to the ground. He wanted to laugh and managed a bubbling hacking cough that turned into dry silent weeping.

A few stall holders ran over. Their feet encircled him, he looked up and saw the same faces that had roared for his destruction and pelted him with rotten fruit.

"Who are you?" they said. "Where did you come from?"

It dawned on him that nobody knew who he was.

The market folk treated him kindly. He was given food and drink, the opportunity to bathe and shave, some old but clean clothes. He refused the shoes, unwilling to put his feet inside the brother and sister of the pair that still sat in the mouth of the cave. Even the memory felt like feeding – something.

"What is your name?"

This was a new life, Mazehew a prisoner who had just noticed his cell door was ajar. Out of deep memory he dredged a name: Alain Edmund Mazehew.

It took a while to regain his strength, his full weight never returned. Alain walked barefoot through the city accompanied by Tobin and Rose, a young couple who sold root vegetables in the market. The petrified gods still brooded in the Avenue of Princes, at night the bearded storytellers and smoke-dancers worked Kala Agr square. The gendarmes at the railway terminus who once fined and arrested him looked through him like he was made of glass.

Alain led Rose and Tobin through the maze of packed earth alleyways to a particular narrow street, a set of apartments, his old room. A young man lived there, a student come to study geology from one of the inland cities.

The student was polite if puzzled. "You used to live here?"

"Not here, but yes, once I did."

The student, Rose and Tobin shared a patient look.

Mazehew pointed to the window. "The frame sticks, you need to thump it on the right."

The student laughed, wondering. "Yes, it does."

That evening, Alain told Rose and Tobin how he had descended from a city almost identical to theirs.

"That was my first life, this is my second. I see you don't believe me. That's all right, I don't deserve belief."

A dilapidated three-walled shack stood on rough ground beyond the market, perhaps seven feet square. Alain borrowed a broom and swept it out. He stuffed some old potato sacks with dry grass and the shack became his home.

Because he was there at night, because he was somehow "theirs', the stallholders called him their watchman and paid him in food. Tobin and Rose gave him a few things – a cup and bowl, a moth-eaten blanket to hang over the open side, a new one to sleep under.

Every morning, Alain walked through the city to the rail terminus. He sat on the steps by the taxi rank and watched the tourists from the morning train. There were fewer here than above, sometimes they asked him for directions and he gladly gave them. Taxi-cabs revved their blue-smoke engines and nut-sellers cried their wares until the crowd thinned.

The city was the same but different, more placid, more sedate. No kite-riders hung off the Edge, no glide-wings soared and dipped. And Frayel did not come.

One day he remembered the orange pips in the pocket of his one-sleeved shirt, the pale desiccated things were the last connection he had to his first life. He planted them in a scrape of soil behind the hut, spaced them carefully and patted down the earth. Water was the easy thing, a freshet trickled from rising ground a hundred feet behind the hut. He tended the seeds for a week, forgot about them for two more and discovered to his delight that most had germinated.

Alain sifted earth from rock with his bare hands and built a series of half-moon terraces on the scrubby slopes around the freshet. There he carefully transplanted the seedlings.

Time passed differently here, the years slid along like days. He cut channels and pools and diverted the freshet around his seedlings and saw them grow into trees. In the heat of the afternoon he sat in their dappled shade and listened to the water flow. On quiet days Tobin and Rose sat with him. Alain talked of his past life as if Mazehew was another person. A few of Tobin's and Rose's friends joined them. One or two returned. Alain gave them oranges; they left him bread, meat, a few pennies.

Everyone had their favourite stories:

"Tell us about the shoe cave."

"Tell us about the glide-wing riders."

"Tell us about the time it rained."

"The old fruit-seller."

One day he recognised the student who lived in his old room. The young man approached, quietly excited. "I built a glide-wing. It works. I flew!"

Happiness blossomed in Alain. "That is – rather wonderful."

The city was changing. All the talk was about air and space, a life lived beyond the Edge. Men and women flew kites from the Grand Parade, a dozen glide-wing workshops were set up in the new quarter, kite sellers opened in the bazaar. Alain still visited the rail terminus every day and watched and waited, hoping without hope.

Rose found him leaning on the wall beside the cauldron. He was no longer scared of the empty gulf, of looking at a sky that reached down forever. They watched the kite-riders spool out on their mile-long lines

"This would never have happened without you," Rose said. "Our city is becoming like yours."

She was right. If Mazehew was here, he would recognise it. Perhaps now Frayel would come.

Rose hesitated, then gathered herself. "You've changed us too, changed me. There's more to life than this one life."

Alain was far away remembering Mazehew and did not hear.

The visitors to the orange grove grew to a crowd, a throng. Tobin, Rose and the student relayed Alain's words to the people at back. Sun bleached his clothes white, he still went barefoot. Those who sat and listened called him 'Pasha'.

Everyone had their favourite story.

"Tell us about the day she fell."

One morning Alain woke and found the market deserted. He sat in the shade of his trees and waited but nobody came, not even Tobin and Rose. Puzzled, he walked into town and found it too was empty except for a handful of puzzled tourists. The bazaars were shuttered, Kala Agr a wide and empty space. The petrified Gods lurked in the rustling silence under the trees of the Avenue of Princes.

Alain cried "Hello". And again, "Hello!" The empty streets grew eerie. Suddenly frightened, Alain hurried back to the orange grove.

Far out along the Edge, movement caught his eye. A dense flock of glide-wings wheeled and dipped high above the distant blue crags.

An offland wind blew steadily towards the Edge. A psychic pressure flowed from the city. Alain watched more and more glide-wings launch and rise.

A black cataract erupted from craggy peaks beneath the flyers, a torrent of water poured out into the air and down through the blue void. The sight bemused Alain, how could a river flow from a peak? Why had it begun? Why was the water so dark? Mystified, he saw how the torrent broke not into mist and spray but discrete specks. Specks like the ones that hung under the glide-wings. Enlightenment came like a dagger-thrust – the cataract and the empty city were one and the same, each explained the other.

The strength went from his legs, he slid to the ground and stared sightlessly through the railings into the endless air. "No." He whispered the word over and again. "No, no, no."

And later, when reason returned: "Why?"

The sun moved; wind pushed through the silent city. Alain became aware of a shadow. A hand pressed on his shoulder and he heard Rose's voice:

"Pasha. What troubles you?"

Alain looked up at her and felt one thousand years old. Tobin offered his hand. Alain clung to them. "I saw…" It was difficult for him to say the words. "I saw…"

He had to look again.

The great cascade had ended. A few glide-wings were still visible. They spiralled up and out in wide graceful curves higher, out to where the air thinned and the wind would fail.

One by one they disappeared and the sky was empty. Alain clutched Rose and Tobin's hands. "You are still here."

"We would never leave without saying goodbye," Tobin said.

"Leave –?"

Rose and Tobin climbed over the railings. Balanced on the Edge, Tobin took Rose's hand.

"Wait," Alain begged.

Tobin looked genuinely puzzled. "Why?"

And they went.

Tourists fled on the last train, the city was utterly deserted. Red rage consumed Alain. This was his doing, he had made the city what it was. If the city was his then he would smash it. There would be no more city.

He flung benches through hotel windows, in the Avenue of Princes he tore branches from the trees. He beat his fists bloody against the petrified

Gods, beat them until he broke his hand. He ran through the silent city destroying until the noises of destruction frightened him and he huddled in shadow.

Night fell, an endless silence of wind and lightless windows. Alain set fires in the rail terminus and the bazaars, in the department stores and hotels along the Avenue of Princes, the cafes of the Grand Parade. In what had once been his own room.

Dozens of plumes of smoke stained the dawn sky. Fires burned through the city but the city would not burn. Alain sat against the railing of the Grand Parade in a stupor of exhaustion. An unlit cigarette hung between his fingers, an empty wine bottle rolled at his feet.

A flock of pterodactyls flew down the length of the Grand Parade towards the distant crags on creaking wings. Soon after they had gone, the morning wind began to blow.

The fires burned stronger. One by one they merged into a red conflagration. Alain watched sheets of fire a hundred feet high tear the air over the city.

The natural wind strengthened as the flames sucked in air. A firestorm grew, a roaring white hurricane. Uprooted trees, chairs and tables flew through the air. Alain tried to run, the gale sucked him towards the fire, he fell and rolled like a rag doll.

Alain clawed his way along the Grand Parade with his elbows hooked through the railings. The heat was terrible, his face scorched, his clothes charred and smoked. In one moment of awful clarity, he watched the hair on his forearm shrivel. After a hundred yards of crawling agony the heat abated, the wind decreased. Streaming smoke, Alain staggered out of the city, past the market and collapsed in his hut.

The city burned through the night, a silhouette of saw-tooth ruins backlit by fire beneath a pall of smoke. In the smoky dawn Alain picked a basket of oranges from his trees and filled a bottle with water from the freshet. He loaded them into the cauldron and climbed in. He shifted his weight, the great cauldron tilted. Clanking and grinding it juddered across stone, slid over the side and sank down, down and down.

3

Mazehew lived in his old room where the window stuck and sold hand-drawn maps to incoming tourists at the rail terminus. In the evenings he sat in the Zapotek café and painstakingly updated his master diagram. Each new edition was more detailed, more accurate.

Every day he sat on the steps of the terminus and watched the crowds. When all the passengers had come down the steps and talked to the taxi drivers or stood looking lost, only when he was absolutely sure did he go down and mingle with them.

"Hello, do you know where to go? May I help?"

"Would you like a map of the city?"

"Do you know the way to your hotel? Let me show you –"

"You are very kind. Here is your change."

A day came when he had a feeling. He turned and there she was, at the top of the steps. Frayel looked around, her gaze swept across his face, hesitated, and moved on.

It was too much. She did not know him, not here. Mazehew made himself sit and watch. When she left, he followed, down through the bazaar, along the Avenue of Princes and out onto the Grand Parade where the wind blew and the sky went on forever.

Frayel drifted to the railing like a sleepwalker. She looked out over the Edge, then down. Her fingers stroked the pocked and weathered ironwork, one foot lifted onto the bottom rail. Mazehew tensed but she stepped back, turned, and wandered along the parade. He followed until he saw a man and woman wearing the white sashes of Guardians.

"Excuse me. I'm worried about that young woman."

The Guardians followed his gaze. "Do you know her?"

Mazehew made a noise in his throat. "We used to be friends."

The Guardians moved between Alain and Frayel. "Thank you. We will speak with her."

The next morning Alain watched Frayel climb the steps up to the terminus accompanied by the two Guardians. She looked exhausted but she smiled and shook their hands. They turned to go; Frayel cried out and flung herself into their arms. Alain watched from the shadows, aching inside.

That evening he drank the best wine at the Zapotek café. The best but not the most expensive. Peace filled him. He left before the smoke dancers came and walked down the Avenue of Princes to the Edge. Stars and constellations shone in the night sky, out and up and also down.

He went back to his room, took his master map and pushed it under the door of the printers.

This he could do for her. As many times as was needed.

With the last of his money, he bought seven oranges.

In the morning he was gone.

Lightning Source UK Ltd.
Milton Keynes UK
UKHW012148210820
368624UK00003B/962

9 781908 125699